The Best Of Today's MOVIE THEMES

Project Manager: TONY ESPOSITO

© 1998 WARNER BROS. PUBLICATIONS
All Rights Reserved

Any duplication, adaptation or arrangement of the compositions
contained in this collection requires the written consent of the Publisher.
No part of this book may be photocopied or reproduced in any way without permission.
Unauthorized uses are an infringement of the U.S. Copyright Act and are punishable by law.

STAR WARS TRILOGY SPECIAL EDITION LOGO: ®, TM and © 1998 Lucasfilm Ltd.

Contents

The Prayer *(Quest For Camelot)* 9

At The Beginning *(Anastasia)* 22

Because You Loved Me *(Up Close And Personal)* 4

Cantina Band *(Star Wars)* 6

Foolish Games *(Batman & Robin)* 8

For You I Will *(Space Jam)* 10

Gotham City *(Batman & Robin)* 12

How Do I Live *(Con Air)* 14

I Believe I Can Fly *(Space Jam)* 16

I Stand Alone *(Quest For Camelot)* 15

The Imperial March *(The Empire Strikes Back)* 18

Journey To The Past *(Anastasia)* 24

Kissing You *(Romeo & Juliet)* 19

Looking Through Your Eyes *(Quest For Camelot)* 20

My Heart Will Go On *(Titanic)* 28

Respect *(Blues Brothers 2000)* 27

Soul Man *(Blues Brothers)* 26

Star Wars (Main Theme) *(Star Wars)* 7

Theme from "UP CLOSE & PERSONAL"
BECAUSE YOU LOVED ME

Words and Music by
DIANE WARREN
Arranged by TONY ESPOSITO

Slowly ♩ = 76

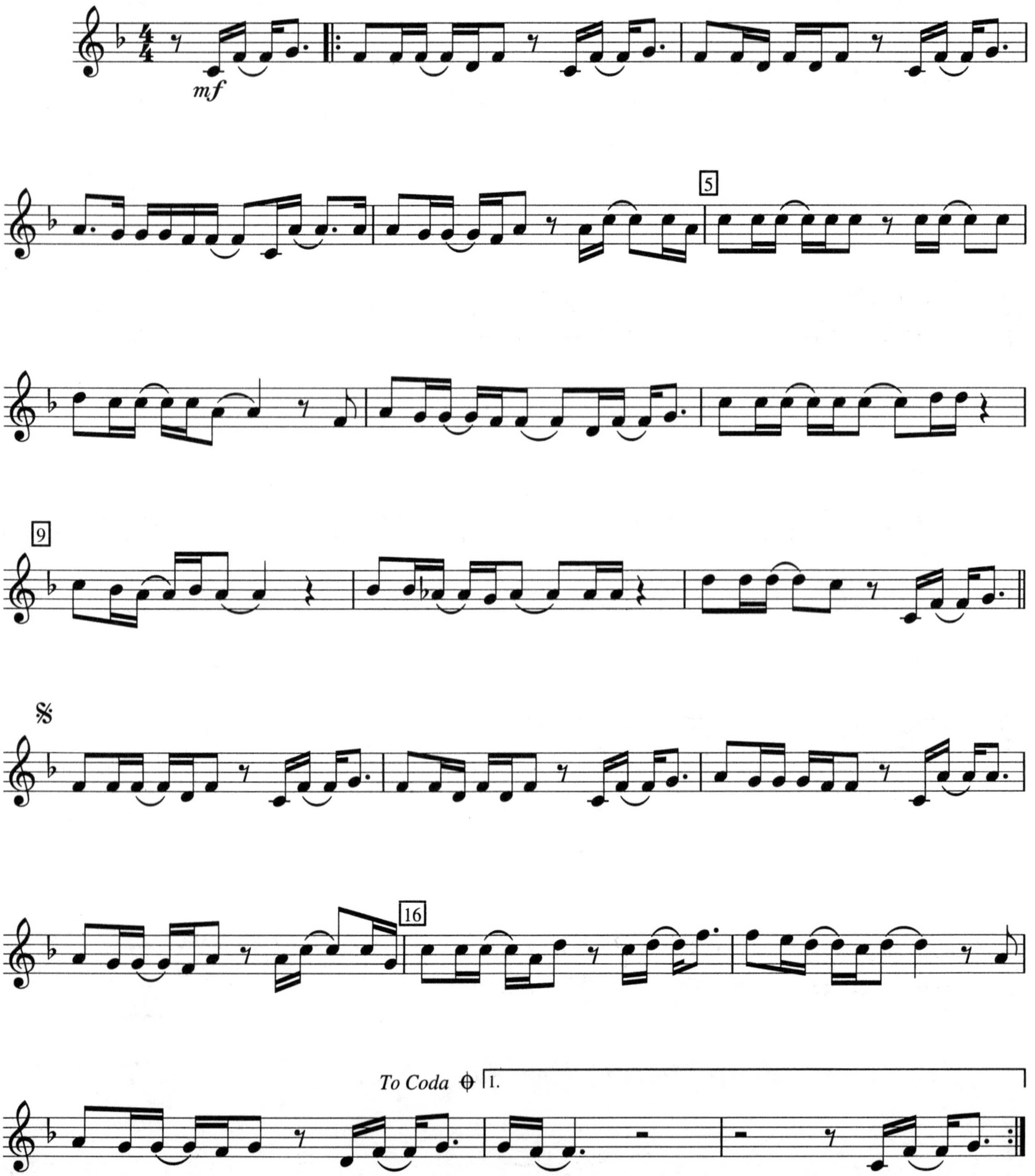

Because You Loved Me - 2 - 1
IF9817

© 1996 REALSONGS (ASCAP)
and TOUCHSTONE PICTURES SONGS & MUSIC, INC. (ASCAP)
All Rights Reserved

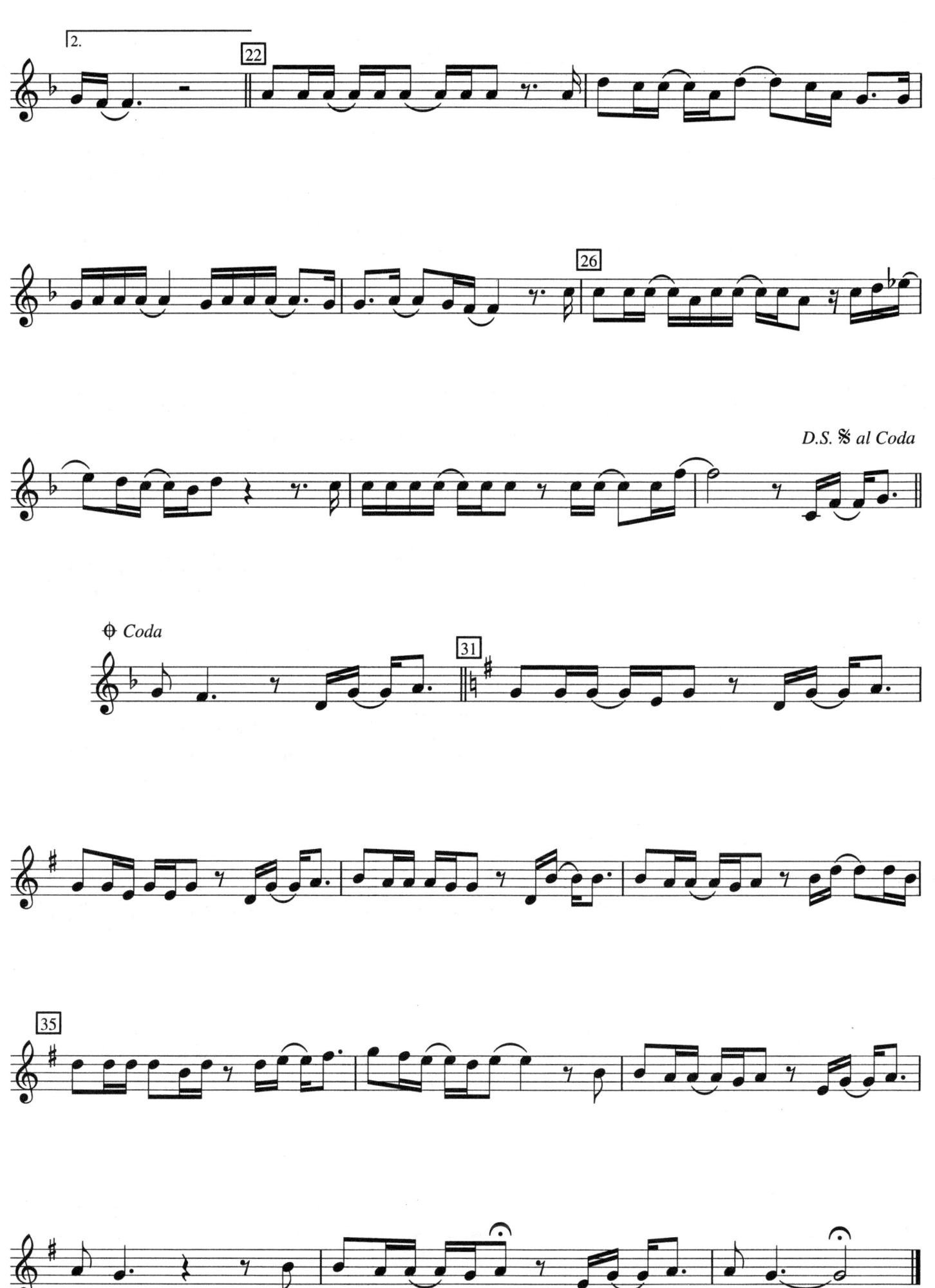

FOOLISH GAMES

By JEWEL KILCHER
Arranged by TONY ESPOSITO

FOR YOU I WILL

Words and Music by
DIANE WARREN
Arranged by TONY ESPOSITO

For You I Will - 2 - 1
IF9817

© 1996 REALSONGS/WB MUSIC CORP. (ASCAP)
All Rights Reserved

GOTHAM CITY

Words and Music by
R. KELLY
Arranged by TONY ESPOSITO

36
mf
40
f
43
47
1.
2.
52
Play 3x
mf

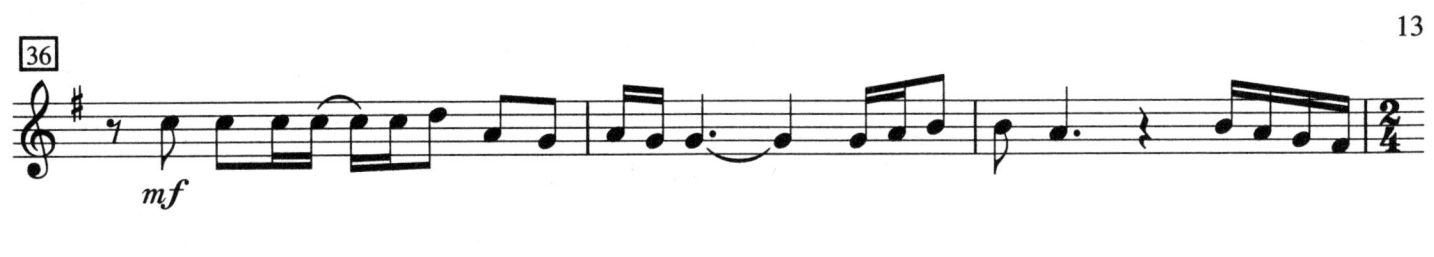

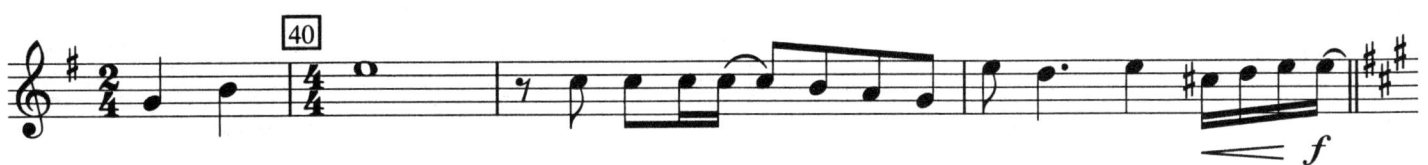

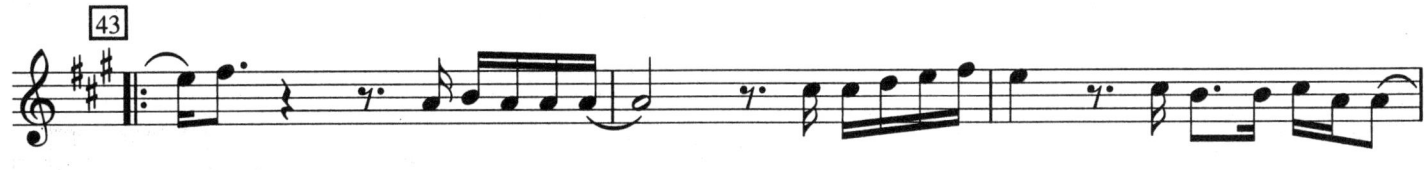

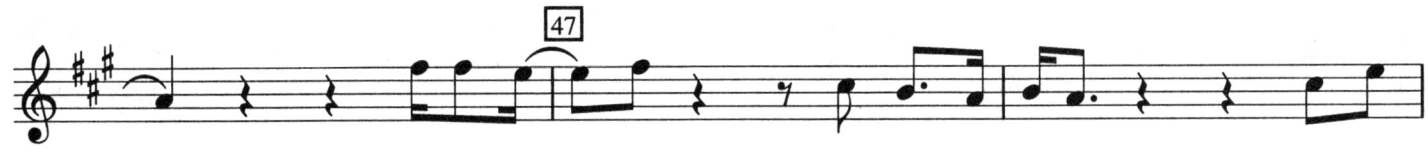

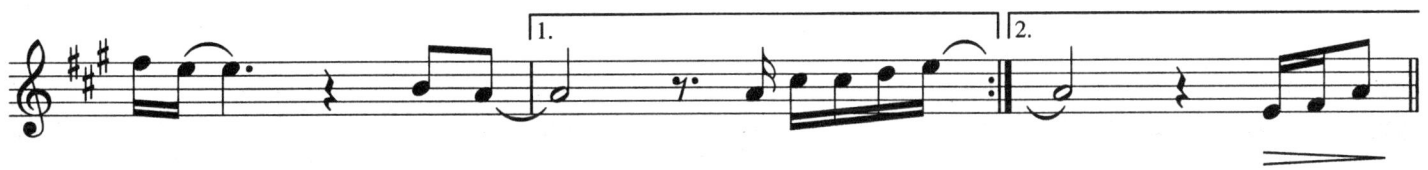

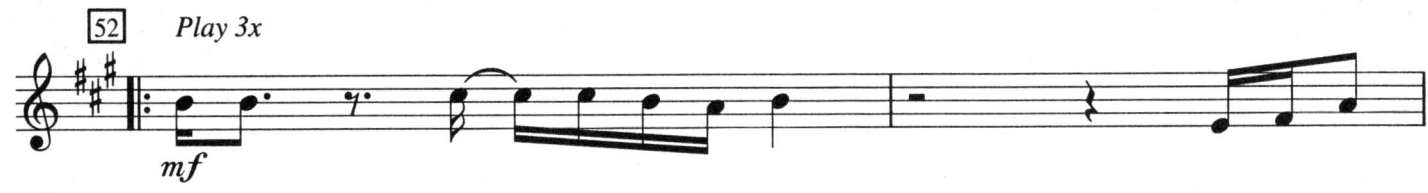

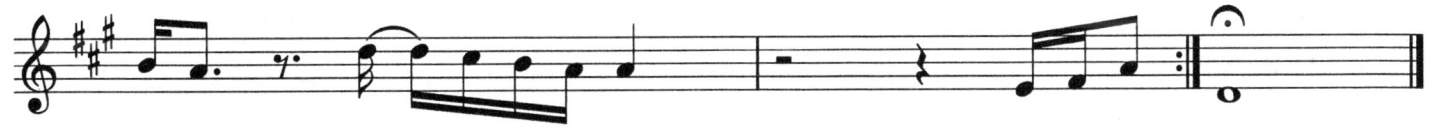

Theme from "SPACE JAM"
I BELIEVE I CAN FLY

Words and Music by
R. KELLY
Arranged by TONY ESPOSITO

I Believe I Can Fly - 2 - 1
IF9817

© 1996 ZOMBA SONGS INC./R. KELLY PUBLISHING, INC. (adm. by ZOMBA SONGS INC.)
All Rights Reserved

From the Twentieth Century Fox Motion Picture "ANASTASIA"
JOURNEY TO THE PAST

Words and Music by
LYNN AHRENS and STEPHEN FLAHERTY
Arranged by TONY ESPOSITO

Journey to the Past - 2 - 1
IF9817

© 1996 T C F MUSIC PUBLISHING, INC. (ASCAP) and FOX FILM MUSIC CORP. (BMI)
This Arrangement © 1998 T C F MUSIC PUBLISHING, INC. (ASCAP) and FOX FILM MUSIC CORP. (BMI)
All Rights Reserved

From "BLUES BROTHERS"

SOUL MAN

Words and Music by
ISAAC HAYES and DAVID PORTER
Arranged by TONY ESPOSITO

From "BLUES BROTHERS 2000"
RESPECT

Words and Music by
OTIS REDDING
Arranged by TONY ESPOSITO